minedition

*published by Penguin Young Readers Group*

Text copyright © 2007 Géraldine Elschner
Illustrations copyright © 2007 Jean-Pierre Corderoch and Eve Tharlet
Original title: Kleines Huhn und Kleine Ente
English text translation by Charise Myngheer
Coproduction with Michael Neugebauer Publishing Ltd., Hong Kong.
Rights arranged with "minedition" Rights and Licensing AG, Zurich, Switzerland.

Published simultaneously in Canada.
Manufactured in China
Typesetting in Goudy Old Style.
Color separation by Fotoreproduzioni Grafiche, Verona, Italy.

Library of Congress Cataloging-in-Publication Data available upon request.

ISBN 978-0-698-40059-7
10 9 8 7 6 5 4 3 2 1
First Impression

For more information please visit our website: www.minedition.com

# Géraldine Elschner Max's Magic Seeds

## with Pictures by
## Jean-Pierre Corderoch

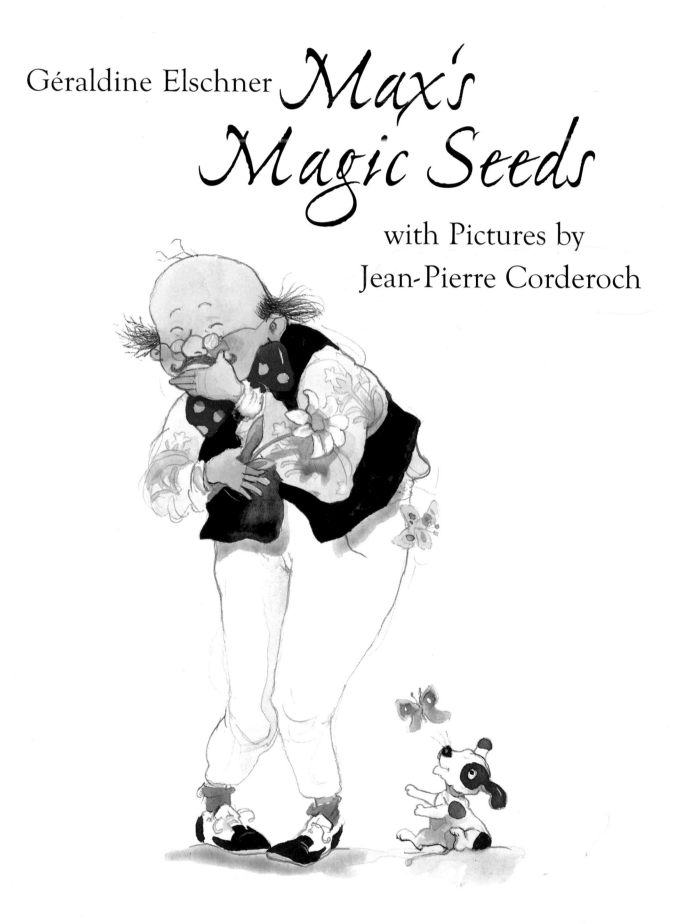

minedition

Translated by Charise Myngheer

My name is Max, and today is my birthday.
That's me sitting by the window, waiting.
All the guests have arrived, except one is still missing—
my favorite uncle, Uncle Bill.
"He's never on time!" complained Aunt Betty.
"Yeah, maybe so," I said.  "But he always shows up."
She knew I was right...
"And he brings the funniest
gifts of anybody!" I added.

Suddenly, a horn honked
loudly, and a really old bus
stopped in front of the house.
"He's here!" I shouted
and ran to the door.

With his bald head and his bow tie, Uncle Bill sort of reminds me of a clown. But actually, he's very well known. He's a botanist— Dad says that means he knows a lot about flowers.

Uncle Bill motioned to me. "Come quick," he said. "I have something for you, but shhh, it's a secret!"

"A secret?" I asked and followed him curiously.

Inside the bus was a large potato sack waiting for me.

"It's huge!" I said in amazement as I untied the knot. "But what is it?"

The sack was full of seeds: big ones, little ones, fat ones, thin ones.

When Uncle Bill saw the confused look on my face,

he laughed so hard that his moustache began to dance!

"Just listen to me," he said, suddenly sounding serious.

"You have to go to school and..."

"Not again," I said as I made a face. "Getting up early

and walking to my boring school is not exactly fun."

"I know," nodded Uncle Bill. "So, I thought of something

you can do to make it more interesting."

"Really?" I said. "How?"

"You can beautify your way to

school!" he said.

"I don't get it," I answered.

"It's simple," Uncle Bill explained. "You now have a bag of flower seeds. You can grow sunflowers, daisies, buttercups, marigolds and a lot more. When you leave the house, you should fill your pockets with the seeds. Then on your way to school you can scatter them everywhere: along the sidewalk, beside the fountain, in front of the school, just anywhere you find soil!"

"Then what?" I asked.

"Then you need to be patient. But be careful," he warned. "Nobody should see you do it. It should be a surprise!"

"Well, if you say so," I said. Then, like two thieves, we snuck into the house and hid the bag in my closet.

The next morning I did as I had promised.
I grabbed a handful of seeds and left for school.
Like always, I was as slow as a snail.
And like always, Mom complained. "Hurry up!"
she said.
"Okay, okay," I said. "I'm coming."
Without being noticed, I scattered my seeds along
the way.

Each morning for almost a week,
I scattered the seeds just as I had promised.
Monday, Tuesday, Wednesday, Thursday
and Friday.
At first nothing happened.
Absolutely nothing.
I began to have my doubts.

But then one day,
I saw some little green spots
between the cracks in the sidewalk.

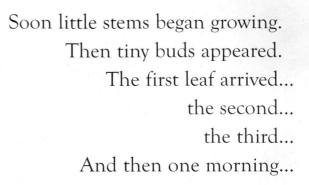

Soon little stems began growing.
Then tiny buds appeared.
The first leaf arrived...
the second...
the third...
And then one morning...

"Oh! How beautiful!"
 said Mom as she saw a poppy next to the sidewalk.
 How do you think it got here—in the middle of the city?"
 she asked. I grinned from ear to ear.
"There must be a little magician running around!"
 I said. "Hocus, pocus.  Flowers bloom!"
 Then I picked the poppy and took it to school.

Mrs. Cummings was so pleased with my poppy that she put it in a vase.
Each day thereafter, I brought a different flower to school.

We looked up all the new flowers in a big book.
Then we painted pictures of them and hung them on the wall.
The classroom began to look great!

Our town also became more interesting. It was as though a colorful ribbon led the way through the streets to the school. Flowers had bloomed everywhere because I had scattered the rest of the seeds beside the parking lot, in front of the mayor's office, and along the bank of the river.

Mrs. Cummings even organized a field trip to go look at all the flowers.

I got to be the guide!

It was a lot of fun, but I never told anyone where they all came from.

The community was more than amazed. "What's going on?" "Unbelievable!" "Beautiful!" No one understood why, but everyone was happy and enjoyed going for walks. Aunt Betty even seemed to be in a better mood.

Then something really unbelievable happened! One day, a letter arrived at City Hall.

It said that our town had won a contest called "The Power of Flowers." To receive the prize, the mayor was supposed to build a stage in the center of the city between the pansies and the forget-me-nots.

As everyone gathered together for the celebration, there was a surprise waiting for me.

In the middle of the mayor's speech, he called my name and asked me to join him on stage.

"I would like to say a special thanks to our
flower magician!" he announced loudly.
"But how did you know?" I asked.
"It was easy to find you," laughed the mayor. "The
flowered path lead directly to your house!"
With a face as red as a poppy, I stuttered into
the microphone, "It was... it was Uncle Bill's present...
When I grow up, I want to be a flower specialist just like him!"
Everyone clapped and cheered for me.  Uncle Bill smiled
proudly at me from the audience.
Then he laughed so hard that his moustache began to dance!